Happy Cat

D1642754

Thunder
the white horse

Thunder, the big white horse that lives in
the field near Martha's school, is old and
cranky and doesn't like being patted.
But in her dreams Martha sees him
quite differently.

Happy Cat First Readers

Thunder
the white horse

Ursula Dubosarsky

Illustrated by Patricia Mullins

HAPPY CAT BOOKS

Published by
Happy Cat Books
An imprint of Catnip Publishing Ltd
14 Greville Street
London EC1N 8SB

First published by Penguin Books, Australia, 2008

This edition first published 2011
3 5 7 9 10 8 6 4 2

A CIP catalogue record for this book is available from the British Library.

ISBN: 978-1-905117-95-6

Printed in India

www.catnippublishing.co.uk

This story first appeared in *The School Magazine*,
published by the New South Wales Department of Education.

In memory of Jerry, for the
children of Ryde East Public School.
U.D.

To Julia, whose dreams of a horse
have never died.
P.M.

Chapter One

Across the road from
Martha's school was a field
with a fence. Behind the
fence was an old white
horse named Thunder.

It wasn't the sort of place
you'd expect to find a field,

or a horse. It was just an
ordinary street with houses
and cars and shops. But
Thunder had been in the
field with his head hanging

over the fence for years,
ever since Martha had been
coming to school, and even
before that.

'Thunder's very, very old,'

said Martha's mother. 'Look
how his ribs stick out, the
poor old thing.'
Sometimes they would

stop on the way home from
school and give Thunder a
carrot.

Thunder would amble
over to them and snatch the
carrot from Martha's hand
with his big brown teeth,

crunching and slobbering.

He wasn't exactly friendly.

'He's too old to be

friendly,' said Martha's

mother.

If Martha was feeling

brave, she would carefully
put up her hand and try
to stroke Thunder's coat while
he chewed on the carrot.
His hair felt hard and thick.
Up close it looked yellow.

But Thunder didn't like
to be stroked. He would
snort and shift and toss
his big head to shake her
off. The sudden movement
made Martha jump back.

'He's just cranky,' said Martha's mother. 'He's so old, that's all.'

Chapter Two

Everyone at school knew
Thunder. Martha and her
mother weren't the only
ones who stopped each day
to talk to him and give him
something to eat.

Lots of children had
cats and dogs at home, or
budgies or goldfish or even

guinea pigs. But there was

something strange and

huge and almost magical

about a white horse, even
an old skinny cranky one
like Thunder.

Sometimes Martha
dreamed about Thunder.
In her dreams, Thunder
wasn't old and cranky and

skinny. He was shining white
and round, and there was a
sort of laugh in his eyes as
he trotted up to her and put

his head over the fence.

'Hallo, Thunder,' Martha
would say.

In her dreams, Thunder
didn't mind being patted.
He seemed to like it.

Martha could even lay her head against his cheek, and Thunder would whinny, gently.

'I love Thunder,' Martha whispered to herself. 'Even if he doesn't love me.'

Chapter Three

At school they had Art.
They could paint whatever
they liked. Martha
painted a white horse on
a background of dark blue
sky. She put some stars in
the sky and a moon. Then

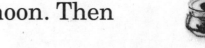

she held her paintbrush
over the top of the painting,
wondering.

'Is that Thunder?' asked
her friend Maddie, looking
over her shoulder.

'I don't know,' said
Martha. 'Maybe.'

She felt embarrassed.
She hid the painting inside
her desk.

Chapter Four

One day after school,
Thunder wouldn't come
over to the fence. He didn't
turn round when any of the
children called out to him.

'Poor old horse,' said
Martha's mother, sighing.

'He really doesn't look well.'

Martha had to hurry
away because she had a
piano lesson. But she didn't
like the piano. She would

much rather have stayed
with Thunder.

Her mother took her to
school next morning in
the car, because they were

running late. There was no time to stop and say hallo to Thunder.

When Martha looked out the car window she could see Thunder way down

at the back of the field,
leaning against a tree. She
had a funny feeling, as
though something inside
her was dropping.

Chapter Five

That night Martha
dreamed about Thunder
again. It was the sort of
dream that you still believe
is true, for a little while,
when you wake up.

In Martha's dream,

school was over for the day.
The bell was ringing but
Martha was already out

the gate. She was standing
alone next to Thunder's
field. There was nobody

else to be seen anywhere,
no cars, no people, only
Martha and Thunder.

'Thunder!' she called out.
'Thunder!'

At the very back of the
field, Thunder turned. He
came galloping towards her.
He looked strong and wild,
and his hoofs beat loudly on
the earth. His mane and his
coat shone like the light of
the moon.

Martha clapped her
hands and laughed.
Then she noticed
something amazing. On
Thunder's back was a pair

of feathery wings! They stretched out under the afternoon sun, quivering like sails on a boat.

'Thunder?' said Martha.

Thunder came up to the
fence. But there was no
fence, not any more.

Martha turned slowly
towards his face and looked
into his black quiet eyes.

Then she woke up. Her
heart was beating so hard!
It wasn't until she had
finished her breakfast that
she was quite sure it was
only a dream.

Chapter Six

When Martha arrived at school that day, everyone was very sad.

'Did you hear what happened?' the children said to each other. 'Thunder died.'

Thunder died. Thunder died. The old white horse was dead.

There was a handwritten

notice pinned to the tree.

After a long life, said the
note, *Thunder has passed
away. Thank you to all his*

friends who made his last

years so happy.

Someone had put flowers

under the tree. Soon there

were more. Pink and yellow

and purple. And more.

Some children left letters
for Thunder. Some left
poems. Everyone was so
sad. How could the dear old
horse be dead?

Chapter Seven

Martha felt like a bottle with nothing left inside it. Not even a drop.

'Poor Thunder,' said her mother. 'Try not to be too sad. He was so old.'

No he wasn't, thought

Martha. She shook her head hard. That's just how he looked, she thought. But that's not how he was, not really. I know how he really was.

She took her painting of the white horse that she had hidden in her desk. She and her mother went over to the field where Thunder used to stand. Even the fence was gone now.

They walked down to
the tree, where people had
left flowers and letters for
Thunder.

Martha's mother had
brought some pins.

Martha pinned the
painting of Thunder on
the trunk of the tree. She
pushed the pins in really
hard.

She must have had
at least one drop left
inside her, because there
were tears in her eyes,
and some of them fell on
her cheeks.

'It's a beautiful painting,
Martha,' said her mother.
'It looks as though Thunder
is flying.'

Martha looked at her
painting. Through her
tears, it was a bit wobbly.
But her mother was right.

To
Thunder

We loved

Thunder was flying, high, high in the far-away sky, on huge white wonderful wings.

From Ursula Dubosarsky

Thunder was a real horse called Jerry. He lived in a field opposite Ryde East Public School in Sydney, where I was working for a while. Jerry was part of the local community such a long time and was very much loved. When he died, the children at the school in particular were very upset. But how beautiful it was to see all the cards and pictures and flowers and letters left for him under his tree. It was all that love that made me want to write this story about him.

From Patricia Mullins

Like Martha in this story, I spent
my childhood dreaming and longing
for a horse to own. While waiting
for this to happen (it never did)
I drew, painted and read about
horses, rode real horses, and spent
all my pocket money on toy horses.
This great love has never left me.

A dream horse can be as 'alive' as
any real horse, so I have drawn
Martha's Thunder as if he is both
magical and real.

If you enjoyed reading *Thunder the white horse*, you can look out for other Happy Cat First Readers...

The Princess and the Unicorn

Wendy Blaxland

No one believes in unicorns any more. Except Princess Lily, that is.
So when the king falls ill and the only thing that can cure him is
the magic of a unicorn, it's up to her to find one.
But can Lily find a magical unicorn in time?

Becky was cross with her little brother. 'If you don't leave me alone,' she said to him, 'I'll put a spell on you!' But she didn't mean to make him disappear!

Crystal longs to be a mermaid.
Her mother makes her a flashing silver tail. But it isn't like
being a proper mermaid. Then one night Crystal wears her
tail to bed...

Jock can make a special sound like a duck!
If you can learn to make it too you can help Jock rescue the
little duck from the duck hunter. Quick, before it's too late!

David's had a party invitation!
It's a dressing-up party and he's going to go as a fox. But
when he arrives he can see he's made a mistake in choosing
his costume. Can he still fit in with the party theme and
have fun?

Nicholas Nosh is the littlest pirate in the world. He's not allowed to go to sea. 'You're too small,' said his dad. But when the fierce pirate Captain Red Beard kidnaps his family, Nicholas sets sail to rescue them!

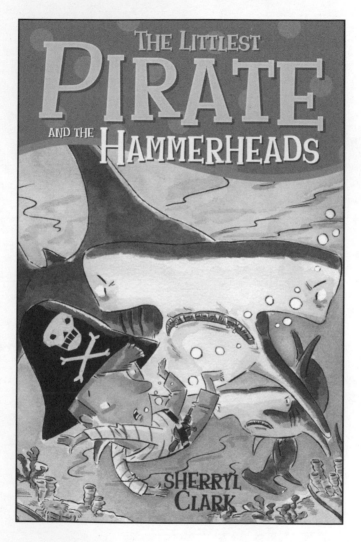

Nicholas Nosh, the littlest pirate in the world, has to rescue his family's treasure which has been stolen by Captain Hammerhead. But how can he outwit the sharks that are guarding Captain Hammerhead's ship?

Nicholas Nosh is teased by his cousin Primrose for being so small. But when Captain Manners of the Jolly Dodger kidnaps her, Nicholas shows just how brave a little pirate he can be!

When Anna
Slept Over

Jane Godwin

Josie is Anna's best friend. Anna has played at Josie's house,
she's even stayed for dinner, but she has never slept over.
Until now...

Tom was given a gorilla suit for his birthday. He loved it and wore
it everywhere. When mum and dad took him to the zoo he
wouldn't wear his ordinary clothes. But isn't it asking for trouble
to go to the zoo dressed as a gorilla?

First day at a new school for Kerry. It's easy to get lost in a big new school when you don't know anyone. But a helpful dog shows Kerry the way to the playground – and to lots of new friends!